Say What You Need to Say

J. Adams

Jewel of the West Publishing

ISBN-13: 978-0615636931
ISBN-10: 0615636934

To Seante',
Our chic, hippie, free-spirited granola girl.
You make us smile!

Knoxville, Tennessee

"Come on, Doc. You've known my family for years. Shoot, as a baby, I even peed on you when you changed my diaper and initiated you into the family, so just say it."

Unsmiling, the older man rubs his temples with his thumb and index finger a moment before meeting my eyes. "Capri, you have ovarian cancer."

Hearing those words completely shifts my world. I am almost twenty years old with my whole life ahead of me. I am just beginning to live, to plan, to dream, to experience. Cancer has never been a part of the plan.

Four days ago the tumor made itself known, and even then, cancer never entered my mind. I mean, young women get benign cysts all the time. Okay, not *all* the time, but it happens, especially–I am told–when it runs in the family.

Both of my grandmothers passed away from ovarian cancer in their later years. They were old and it just happened.

Still, it isn't supposed to happen to me.

My parents are what people classify as free-spirited granola naturalists. All of my mother's prenatal care was given by a midwife and the births were all home water births. We are one of the healthiest families I know. Dad's Catawba Indian ancestry passed down fifty different ways to use corn, and Mom brought her island cooking skills when she immigrated from Jamaica. Twenty-five years in the states and she still speaks with a strong Jamaican brogue, especially when she's angry or upset.

Living on a ranch my whole life, my four older brothers and I were raised on natural everything–raw milk, whole grains, organic vegetables we grow ourselves, fresh eggs laid by our own chickens, beef from our cattle, bacon and pork from our pigs, herbs grown in our greenhouse–so unhealthy eating is definitely not the cause of the disease living inside me. It is genetics.

Through an emotional haze I listen to the man I've known as Uncle Jake all my life go over the hysterectomy procedure and treatment afterward. He says my healthy lifestyle is definitely in my favor and recovery will most likely be quick, and hopefully, permanent. Still, my brain translates his words into one repeated line:

I will never be able to have a baby.

I am sent to a counselor down the hall who gives me a packet of information and suggestions for coping with the coming changes. With her red bouffant hair, flared skirt and pink cat-frame glasses, it's hard to take her seriously. I figure it must be fifties week around the office, possibly a morale booster. As she counsels me to face this ordeal head on, I bite back a sarcastic retort of, "What else am I going to do, close my eyes and wait for it to go away?" But I know she is only doing her job and I do appreciate the information.

I walk out of the medical building feeling like a completely different person. I know my life will soon change. It is inevitable and I accept this.

No counseling needed.

Three months later.

*R*unning a hand over the soft stubble sprouting from my scalp, I tie a pink scarf over it and put on my old, worn black western hat. Having finished the final round of chemo last month and being declared cancer free, my energy level is finally through the roof again and I am anxious to get out and help Dad with the animals. Until now, the most I have been able to do is help Mama a little in the garden and do some light housework–things that she has handled alone for the past while. I am looking forward to feeling useful again.

Taking a final look in the mirror and still feeling unsatisfied with my reflection, I take off the hat and scarf, deciding to don one of my wigs instead. I straighten the long locks on my head and force my mouth to curve into a satisfied smile before heading down to the kitchen for breakfast. Mama turns from the stove and smiles as she places a platter of sausage and bacon on the table to join the eggs and waffles. And just like clockwork, the screen door opens and slams shut and my dad and brothers file in, making a beeline for the table. Seth, the oldest, pulls out my chair just like always, seating me next to himself.

"Thanks," I say, then repeat the usual line, "You know, some lucky woman is out there just waiting for you to find her."

He grins and drapes an arm around my shoulders, giving me his usual reply of, "If she's as fine as you, I will find her soon enough."

I smile, nudging him playfully. I love all of my brothers like crazy, but I've always been closest to Seth. I suppose it's because he has always been the most protective of me, allowing me to tag along wherever he went when I was younger and watching out for me. The whole cancer thing has been worse on him than anyone else. I tell him frequently he's like a mother hen at times and he always replies with a grin and an imitated chicken cluck.

When everyone is seated, I am surprised to hear the screen door open and close again. I look at Seth.

"That will be Jagger," he tells me. "He started a couple of weeks ago."

"Yes," Mama says, "and I've finally talked the man into joining us for breakfast from now on. Since he's the only worker staying in the bunkhouse, it only makes sense. Besides, it's got to be pretty lonely in that place, and this will save him from having to eat breakfast alone."

I smile. Mama never could stand the thought of anyone being alone. "I'm sure he appreciates . . ." I pause as heavy booted footsteps draw closer.

"Morning, Jagger," Dad says and I turn, my heart skipping a beat as I watch the man approach and take the empty seat on the other side of me.

"Mornin'," the handsome cowboy replies, but his smile is definitely for me.

I give him a timid smile in return and quickly look away, telling myself there is no point in showing any interest. Though I am well again, I still don't feel whole, at least not whole enough to have a normal future with anyone. I am sure the moment I return someone's interest and they learn of the cancer and what it took from me, that interest will quickly flee, leaving a fresh scar to join the others. And I can't let that happen.

"Jagger," Seth says, "this is our sister, Capri. Capri, meet Jagger Colby."

"Pleased to meet you, Capri," he says with a deep,

alluring drawl and gray eyes warm enough to heat the coldest of women.

"Nice to meet you." I turn my attention to my food and try to keep it there while conversation and discussions about things pertaining to the ranch flow around me. At one point, I briefly glance at Jagger, unexpectedly meeting an intense gaze that is completely alluring and dangerous to my peace of mind. With his dark tousled waves and muscular physique, he's beautiful, and utterly perfect, which only strengthens my resolve to keep my guard up. My emotions are locked in a vault as big as Fort Knox. And they will stay there.

Yeah, you keep telling yourself that . . . I quickly squash any and all thoughts of failure. Lifting my glass, I take a drink of milk, grimacing as I swallow. "Daddy, it might be just me, but there is something wrong with this milk."

"What do you mean?"

"It just doesn't taste right."

Everyone else pours a little of the milk to sample, simultaneously making faces. I watch Jagger take a drink, smiling at his expression. Even grimacing, he's still gorgeous.

"Sir, no offense, but this milk tastes like it's been sittin' in a liquor bottle. Either that or it's from an alcoholic cow."

I release a very unladylike snort, drawing a grin from the

handsome cowboy, and before I can stop, laughter bubbles to the surface. I glance at Daddy's face and laugh even harder. Pretty soon the roar of everyone's laughter fills the kitchen. Grabbing a napkin, I wipe my eyes, but one more glance at Daddy as he takes another drink from his glass sends me into another fit and I'm holding my side. I haven't laughed this much in a long time.

"Let me check something," Daddy says, getting up from the table. He grabs the phone and jabs at the numbers.

"Hey, Chrispin, it's James. How are ya?" Pause. "Good, yeah, we're doing okay, but I've got a question for ya. That worker you fired last month. Describe him to me." Pause. "Little guy with gray stringy hair, bushy brows, glasses, and he walks with a limp, huh?" Pause. "Well, since my two milking cows are drunk, I'd say I hired the son-of-gun." Daddy shakes his head and rolls his eyes. "Yeah, laugh it up. I took some milk over to the neighbors this morning for her two little boys. Ain't no telling what it'll do to those little hellions. But then again, their mama might thank me."

Jagger leans over and whispers to me, "I've seen them boys rippin' up the place over there. What you wanna bet their mama don't bring her jug over for a refill?"

I snort again and cover my mouth, but a giggle escapes anyway. "I have to agree. Just watching them over there makes me exhausted."

"Yeah, them boys are a couple of tornadoes in a can. It's a wonder that house is still standin'. And I could swear I saw them catapultin' a cat the other day. I could hear the poor thing screechin' clear across the field."

"And you didn't try to rescue it?" I ask with feigned concern, a brow arched.

"Shoot, no! I ain't that crazy." The sexy cowboy lowers his voice and leans closer. "But if you wanna accompany me over there and hold my hand, I just might brave it."

When Seth snickers, heat rushes to my cheeks. "I'm sure my brother would be happy to help you out."

"Naw, darlin'," Jagger says with a chuckle. "Them boys get a look at his ugly mug and I'm a goner. But I know I'd be completely safe with you."

Smiling, I tell him, "I'll think about it." Then I focus my attention on Daddy's phone call.

"And how long did it take for the liquor to go through old Flossie's system?" he asks. "Okay. Thanks, Chrispin. I guess I should have known something was up from the beginning. Nobody smells like mouthwash all day long. The day I hired him, he must have been swigging every few minutes." He's silent for another moment. "I'm going out there to give him the boot right now. Thanks again."

Daddy shakes his head as he hangs up the phone. "I guess I'd better go on and get it done. Ya'll best not drink anymore of that spiked milk."

"I don't know," Mama says. "I think we should freeze it til Christmas and use it for the homemade eggnog we give to friends. What do you think?" She laughs when daddy just shakes his head and leaves. "I guess he didn't think it was funny."

I smile, taking my plate to the sink. "Oh, you know Daddy. Just give him a few days."

After breakfast, Seth and I decide to take a couple of the horses out for some exercise. I've really missed riding and have been looking forward to it for months.

"I'm excited to get back in the saddle," I tell my brother.

"I know," Seth says, handing me my horse's reins. "Capri's Lady has been missing you."

"And I've missed her." I brush a gloved hand down the gray mare's nose. Daddy gave me Capri's Lady when I turned sixteen and she means the world to me. She has been my best friend–yes, my best friend is a horse–and she has always been there for me. Whenever I've gone for rides, I've shared my innermost thoughts with Capri's Lady. She's a great listener.

As we leave the stable, Jagger passes by, tipping his hat to me on his way to the barn.

"Awww, dang it!" Seth says, startling me. "I forgot to make an important phone call this morning. I'm sorry, Capri, but I've gotta go take care of that."

"I can wait for you," I tell him.

"Naw, don't do that." He looks toward Jagger's retreating form and I mouth, *no!* And of course, he ignores me. "Hey, Jagger!"

I turn to my brother, giving him my *You are dead to me!* glare. If I could shoot fire from my eyes, he would be as charred as one of Daddy's burgers after falling into the grill during the Super Bowl.

"Would ya mind filling in for me and going for a ride with Capri?"

"Naw, I don't mind at all," he calls, heading back.

I clinch my jaw and whisper, "You are so in trouble, brother!" Taking a deep breath I force a smile as Jagger approaches. "Thanks, but if you're busy, I don't want to keep you," I tell the painfully-handsome cowboy.

"Oh, I'm never too busy for you, darlin', and you can *keep* me for as long as you want."

Seth snickers and I want to punch him. I've never wanted to inflict bodily harm on someone so much. Jagger slips by me to take the reins of my brother's horse and an unwanted warmth fills me as his body grazes mine.

"Don't you worry none, Seth," Jagger says, intently staring at me, the familiar alluring grin on his face. "I'll take good care of her."

"Don't I know it?" Seth winks at me and takes off toward the house, leaving me wondering what I've gotten myself into.

I'm going to kill him! I'm going to kill him, and then revive him and kill him again!

"I can read that look," Jagger says with a wide smile. "Don't be too mad at him. He probably saw me meltin' over you at breakfast and wanted to help this old boy out a bit. He could see how pathetically gone I was over you the minute I walked into that kitchen. Don't get mad at him for trying to help me out of my misery."

He's done it to me again. Laughter bubbles to the surface before I can stop it, making his smile ever wider. "So, what you're saying is you've been in cahoots with each other the entire time. Is that what I'm hearing?"

"Well, since you put it that way, yeah."

"I love your honesty."

"I love it, too. I'm glad you are impressed."

"And your humility is astounding."

"Ain't it, though?"

There is just no way I can keep a straight face with this

13

man. "Okay, I think we should ride."

"I'm ready when you are, beautiful."

A warm blush heats my face and I immediately turn away from him. Truthfully, I don't feel beautiful. I haven't felt even remotely attractive for a long while now. With a gentle hand, Jagger turns me to face him. His gray eyes are warm as he stares into mine. Then his hands circle my waist and he lifts me, placing me on Capri's Lady. The action leaves me speechless. I have always mounted a horse by stepping up into the stirrups unassisted.

"Thank you," I manage to say.

"You're welcome," he says back, climbing onto his horse. "All right, you just lead the way."

$\mathcal{W}$e ride side by side across the grassy acres at an easy
pace. Surprisingly, I am pretty comfortable and at ease with
Jagger. Maybe it's just the sensation of the longed-for breeze
blowing against my skin, or finally feeling in control of my
life that is bringing me such peace. Whatever the reason,
riding with Jagger is quite enjoyable and conversations flows
freely.

Since Jagger is now at my mercy, I grill him about
himself, asking him everything I can think to ask. And he
answers my questions as quickly as I ask them: He was born
and raised in Alabama and his family is still there. He has
four younger sisters. I know from his birth date that he is
thirty. He's never been married or in a serious relationship
with anyone. When his grandfather passed away six months

15

ago, Jagger inherited his grandfather's cabin rental business, which included a large, furnished resident cabin his grandfather never used. It's currently occupied by a woman who is managing the rentals for him, but she will be leaving in a month. Until then, Jagger will be working for Daddy.

Coming to the old barn near the edge of the property, sitting amidst a shady grove of trees, we stop and rest the horses for a bit. I've always loved spending time here and had actually come to the old place the day before my surgery. Until today, I hadn't been back.

But how did he know about this place?

"Your brother told me this is your favorite spot," he says, seeming to read the question in my eyes.

"It always has been," I agree as he helps me down from my horse, his strong hands lingering on my waist, his gaze holding mine a moment.

Taking a deep breath, I shake my head slightly and struggle to control the heat filling my insides by mentally cooling myself off with an imagined splash of cold water. *Very* cold water. I open the barn door and watch the sunlight slice through the darkness, illuminating a few cobwebs.

Jagger stands aside. "After you." A mischievous grin spreads across his face. "Or would you rather I go first, you know, just in case there are spiders hangin' around waitin' for ya?"

I place closed fists on my hips. "Are you calling me a sissy?"

"Oh, I wouldn't dare." He takes off his hat and leaves it on the saddle pommel. "If anything, it's me who needs protectin' from them little critters. On second thought, you go first."

"Coward," I say with a smile.

"Dang straight."

I laugh. "I appreciate that you are man enough to admit it."

"Honey, I'll admit to anything for the chance to be alone with you in the dark."

My face warms. "Do you even have a tactful bone in your body?"

"Not when I see somethin' I want."

The sultry tone of his answer causes my heart to thump in a way it never has. I clear my throat and enter. Smiling, I walk to the center of the barn.

"Don't laugh, but I've always called this my dream studio," I tell him, lifting my arms and turning. "Oh, I've missed this place!" I smile up at the small beams of sunlight shining through the small cracks in the roof. Unable to help it, I giggle. "Don't you just love it?" When he doesn't answer,

I turn back to him, meeting his silent smile. "What?"

"Nothin," he says shaking his head. "It's just . . . I ain't never in my life seen anything as beautiful as you."

I roll my eyes. "Do you ever stop?"

He takes his hat off and pushes his fingers back through the dark waves. "Well, truthfully I don't know. This is the first time I've ever lost my heart, so you might wanna hold onto it carefully, darlin."

For a moment, I am utterly speechless "But Jagger . . . you don't even know me."

Giving me a slow smile that is almost my undoing, he moves closer and takes my hand. "Don't worry about that, sugar. I've got time and I ain't going nowhere. Besides, I have Seth's seal of approval and his permission to do everything in my power to sweep you off your feet." He squeezes my hand. "And there ain't nothing you can say to scare me off, so just nip that kind of thinkin' in the bud right now. And, yeah, I know that's what's goin' through your mind."

"What has my brother told you about me?" My calm voice belies the worry filling me.

"You mean besides the obvious? That you're beautiful, smart and funny, you love horses and old abandoned barns?"

"Yes," I say with a forced smile, "besides that."

"Well, he said you'd been sick, but you're better now,

which means you're up to some serious datin'–with me, exclusively."

Releasing a relieved chuckle, part of me is a little disappointed that Seth hasn't told him. *It would be better if he already knew. Then again, if he finds out . . . Wait, why in the world am I contemplating this anyway?* Heaving a deep sigh, I admonish myself to enjoy the attention while it lasts . . . because it won't for long.

With his gentle tug on my hand, I find myself in the circle of his muscular arms, pressed against his solid chest. Other than Daddy and my brothers, I have never been this close to a man, and I to say I am tense is an understatement.

"Relax," he whispers against my ear. "I just wanna hold you, honey. That's all."

Allowing myself to soften, my body practically melts against his, soaking in the warmth and gentleness of his embrace. Instead of berating myself for this futile action, I close my eyes and soak in the wondrous comfort that almost brings tears to my eyes. I finally pull away.

"We should probably be heading back."

"Okay" he drawls. "But I do believe I've made some progress."

"You think so, huh?" I smile, amused and completely charmed by his determination to win my affections.

And darn him, it's working!

𝒲e decide to take the long way back. Lost in thought,

I quietly ponder Jagger's words and actions this morning. The man is definitely persistent, I'll give him that. And it is his persistence that makes him so endearing. I casually allow my eyes to travel over his rugged features. He's beautiful, but not in a pretty boy way, and perfectly imperfect.

He surprises me by turning and smiling, meeting my admiring gaze with his own. Neither of us say anything. Words would only be in the way right now because everything that needed saying was said in the barn.

Our ride brings us to an area where our property borders the neighbor's place–home to the two terrors. We can hear the wild boys at play. Holding a finger to his lips, Jagger gets down from his horse. He quickly helps me down, and taking my hand, quietly pulls me over to the tree-lined picket fence. He squats down and peers through a crack.

"Come on down here and check this out," he whispers. I kneel next to him and look through another crack, and the sight before us causes me to smack a hand over my mouth and muffle the bubbling laughter. Jess and James Kenley are on one end of their homemade seesaw with a fat cat strapped to the other end. Since both boys are donning fresh scratches on their arms, it's obvious the cat hadn't intended to go down without a fight and it is still howling in protest.

"That poor cat!" I whisper.

"Yeah, good thing it has nine lives."

"True, but it's probably on its last one." Jagger releases a low snort, which makes it harder for me to keep quiet.

"Watch this." Cupping his hands around his mouth, he makes a noise that sounds like the combination of a coyote and a dinosaur. Both boys jump, looking toward the fence. We laugh at their reaction, as well as the conversation that follows.

"What do you think it was, Jess?"

"Heck if I know," James says. "But I'm gonna find out."

James is walking toward the fence when Jagger repeats the sound, only louder, and the boy stumbles to a stop. "Come over here with me," he tells Jess.

"No way!"

"Fine! I'm gonna see what it is."

Jagger's Tyrannosaurus coyote call comes out as a roar this time and both boys yell and take off toward the house, leaving the poor cat strapped to the seesaw. We both laugh so hard, we double over, falling back in the grass, tears streaming down our cheeks. We try to stop, but another fit hits us and we're soon curled on our sides facing each other. My sides ache, but I couldn't ask for a better pain.

"You are crazy!" I say when I can finally catch a breath.

"True, but I can't remember a time when that particular skill was used on two more deserving 'hellions' as your Daddy called them."

"Well, you are just full of hidden talents, aren't you?"

"Oh, the hidden mysteries for you to discover!"

"Really?" I finally stand and smack the grass from my jeans. Jagger does the same. When he casually reaches out to pick a couple of blades of grass from my hair, it takes serious restraint to keep from flinching. He doesn't know I'm wearing a wig and I definitely don't want him to find out now. I give him my best lazy smile. "I can tell this is going to be fun."

"Darlin', you ain't seen nothin' yet."

During the following weeks, Jagger is true to his word and there is never a dull moment, because nearly every waking moment is spent together. We stay busy during the day with work around the ranch, and no matter what Jagger is doing, he always finds things close by for me to do to help, including milking the two cows. We joke about giving them liquor every now and then to keep breakfast interesting, and maybe keep the neighbor supplied with sedation for Jess and James. Jagger says he needs to be near me and adds in a simpering drawl that he can't function unless I'm there for him to look at.

When the work day is done, I always change into my usual attire: long, billowy Bohemian skirts, lacy tank tops and crocheted shrugs, long beaded necklaces, and ballerina flats. I've always dressed this way and it makes me feel feminine. The first time Jagger comes to the house to pick me up and take me out to dinner, he grins and says, "I'm datin' a beautiful hippie."

I jab him with my elbow. "I am *not* a hippie! Being a hippie makes me think of drugs and free love."

He takes my hand. "Well, while I'm glad you don't do the drug thing, the free love is somethin' I could work with."

"Jagger, I swear, you are impossible!"

"And you wouldn't want me any other way, would ya?"

Looking into his eyes I shake my head no. I wouldn't want him to be any other way, because Jagger says with sincerity, exactly what I need to hear–what every woman needs to hear.

Most evenings we sit on the bunkhouse steps and talk of everything we can think to talk about. He is excited about taking over his grandfather's cabin rental business and he wants to take me to see it, but somehow there always seems to be a reason for me not to go. I know it disappoints him, but he never lets it show, just always assures me there will be a next time.

I spend the time we are away from one another pondering my plight regarding my fear of him discovering the secret I'm keeping from him. Mama says I should just come straight out and tell him. She doesn't think it will make a difference. But I keep telling myself it doesn't matter if I *don't* tell him because soon he will be gone and no longer in my life.

This is what I tell myself.

Over and over.

The thing is, I'm beginning to have a hard time listening.

In all this time, not once has Jagger kissed me, or even tried. He is content to just hold me or take my hand in his. I am a little disappointed because I know just one touch of his lips against mine would be the most heavenly thing I've ever experienced. But I also accept that it is probably for the best. It will be easier on my heart. And yes, despite my efforts to keep my seesawing emotions at bay, my heart is completely involved now, and utterly his. Truthfully, he claimed it the moment we met. I just couldn't admit it.

I couldn't admit it then, and I can't let myself admit it now.

Mama and Daddy have been urging us along. Daddy wants me to be happy and thinks Jagger is just the guy to give me that happiness. Mama feels the same. None of my brothers have married. And while Seth and his girlfriend finally became engaged last week, Paul, Michael and Greer seem to be floundering. They date, but none of them have developed a serious relationship with anyone, which is driving Mama batty. She wants grand kids and has been very vocal about it. And deep down, I'm sure she sadly reminds herself that none will come from me.

I need no such reminder.

Jagger

Lord, I love this woman. And I don't need to hear her say the words to know she loves me. I know it as sure as I'm sittin' here. But she's holdin' back. Why is she holdin' back?

You could say Jagger lost his heart to Capri the moment he walked into his boss' kitchen and saw her, but that is not when it happened. No, Jagger lost his heart the day he was hired and had caught a glimpse of her relaxing on the back patio with a glass of lemonade, reading a book. Her hair was pulled back in a ponytail and she was wearing a wide brimmed hat and sunglasses. Dressed in a peach-colored sundress and gold gladiator sandals, she was the most beautiful thing he had ever seen. He was completely awed and couldn't pull his gaze away. When Seth caught him staring at his sister, Jagger thought he would be fired for sure. But that didn't happen either.

Instead, Seth told him what an amazing person Capri was. And over that first week, Jagger bombarded Seth with questions. He learned everything he possibly could about Capri: She was an avid reader, she loved animals, horseback riding, and summer rain. She loved children, picnicking, watching sappy movies and a good steak.

That week, Jagger fell in love with the woman he had yet to officially meet. But in some ways he'd felt as if he already knew her. Every day, he would watch and wait, longing for a glimpse of her, if only for a moment. Then he was invited to the house for breakfast, and his whole universe shifted.

Before Jagger left Texas, his mother and sisters bugged him constantly about finding a wife. His mother wanted grand kids and his sisters wanted nieces and nephews. And they all cried when he left.

But his father understood him and had given Jagger his blessing, telling him his future bride was just around the corner. And he had been right.

Jagger has never felt about anyone the way he feels about Capri. The love he harbors for her is a shock to his system that will never fade.

He has always been a bold man when it comes to going

after what he wants, but he is also a God-fearing man, and he recognizes that every good thing he has ever had came from God. Surely God would gift him with the love of this woman who has come to mean more than anything in the world.

"I need her, Lord," Jagger softly mumbles, drawing his thoughts to the present as he opens his truck door for Capri. She is wearing the peach sundress and hat, and suddenly every coherent thought leaves him, his senses tuned in to nothing at the moment but being with her.

"Woman, you make my mouth water just lookin' at you!" Her responding smile is warm, but it doesn't reach her eyes.

She's holding somethin' inside, and until she lets it go, I can't have her whole heart. Shaking his head, he pushes the thought from his mind.

Capri gives him the picnic basket she packed for their lunch in the park and climbs up on the seat. Then she gives him another smile, a genuine one this time, and his insides melt all over again.

Lord, I need her like I need air to breathe.

In a couple of weeks, Jagger will be leaving.

But he isn't planning to leave alone.

At least he prays he won't.

*S*itting on a blanket with my back against a shady tree, Jagger stretches out and rests his dark head in my lap. His eyes are closed and I allow myself to gazed down at his relaxed face, then travel the length of his body. One of his large hands holds mine against his chest and I feel his strong heartbeat.

Oh, how I want him, God! I want to be his, to belong to him and him to me. I have never wanted, no, needed, something so much in my life.

I've fought these feelings harder than I have ever fought against anything, but it has been a futile battle. And now I don't know what to do. Sighing, my mind drifts to the the conversation I had with Seth the day I met Jagger. It was after Jagger and I said goodnight and he'd headed down to the bunkhouse.

"I've never had someone come after me so aggressively. Wait, what am I saying? I've never had anyone come after me at all!"

"Well, that's because you are so intimidating."

"Yeah, right."

"I'm serious, Capri. You don't realize just how amazing and beautiful you are. That's a lethal combination and it intimidates men."

"But not Jagger."

"Shoot, nothing intimidates Jagger. And when it comes to you, he will do anything, be anything, whatever it takes to earn your heart. So I guess in a way you do intimidate him." Seth squeezes my hand. *"You place too little value on yourself, Capri. It's not like you."*

I give him a sad smile. "I guess I've forgotten what the real me feels like." Heaving a deep sigh, I brush a tear from my cheek.

"Then let Jagger into your heart and he will help you remember. Stop being afraid."

"That's easier said than done."

I pull my mind back to the present.

Jagger opens his eyes, staring into mine. "Where are you, darlin'?"

"I'm here," I say, brushing a gentle hand over his deep waves. I love his hair. It's incredibly soft and smells great for a ranch worker. Actually, he smells great, period. I mentioned that one day and he said, "I might work on a ranch, but I don't want to smell like it." I told him I wouldn't mind the horse and leather mixture. He promised to keep that in mind. He has the greatest sense of humor. And while many people would consider his vanity a fault, I love it because it is so *him*.

He's perfect for me, I admit for the thousandth time. Next to Daddy and my brothers, I don't think there is a better man.

Jagger reaches up and softly caresses my cheek, trailing a thumb over my lips, and a strong urge to kiss him sweeps over me, causing my face to warm. The catching of his breath and the intensity of his gaze increases the staccato rhythm of my heart, causing it to speed up a few notches. His hand moves to the back of my neck, and just as I begin moving down, a soccer balls hits the side of his head and I chuckle. The moment is gone, but this is priceless.

"Sorry, Mister," a small boy calls on his way over to us.

"That's okay, buddy," Jagger says, sitting up. He hands the boy the ball. "I'll bet you're quite the soccer player."

"I am," the boy says proudly. "My daddy said I'm the best there is."

"And I'm sure your daddy's right."

"Yeah, me and him practice a lot."

"Do ya?"

As I listen to the conversation between Jagger and the little boy, I force a smile to hide the pain in my heart. Looking at them together, all I can think is Jagger would make a great father. As loving and attentive as he is, any child of his would be blessed.

But that can never happen if he chooses a future with me. He would miss out on one of God's greatest gifts.

"It's been good talking to ya," Jagger tells the boy.

"You too, Mister. See ya."

"See ya." Jagger chuckles. "Cute kid, ain't he?"

I smile, managing to blink back the tears pressing. "Jagger, could you take me home now?" I glance at his puzzled expression and look away.

"Why? Are you all right?"

"Yes, I just remembered something I need to do. I'm sorry, but I really need to get back."

"All right." His eyes search my features and I sense his disappointment. I want to apologize again, but I don't think it would make a difference. Saying nothing, we pack everything in the basket and head back to the ranch.

*O*nce I am back home, I thank Jagger and get out of the truck without looking at him. I can't bring myself to because of the pain I am sure his eyes hold. Entering the house, I head straight to my room, unable to face anyone until I get my emotions under control. But no matter how hard I try to keep them at bay, the tears continue to press. I know once I start crying, I won't be able to quit, and then everyone will want to know what's wrong. I can't handle the questions right now.

Changing into a pair of jeans and a light blouse, I pull on my boots and head out to the stable to take Capri's Lady out for a ride, all the while hoping I won't run into Jagger. Seeing him would be too much at the moment.

* * *

Riding away, I finally let the tears come, and they come

in torrents.

I love him, Lord. I love him so much, but I can't have him.

A moment later the sky opens up, releasing a heavy rain. I know I should turn around and head back, but I can't. Not right now. Since the barn is close, I keep going. Then I hear someone calling me in the distance.

It is Jagger.

He saw me leave after all.

Instead of slowing, I keep going until I reach the barn. Jagger arrives right behind me, but I can't bring myself to look at him. I slide down from the horse and lead her inside. He follows and leaves his horse tethered to a post in the corner beside Capri's Lady.

Standing in the center of the barn, I keep my back to him, still unable to look at him.

"Talk to me, Capri." He touches my shoulder and I move away. "Capri, please talk to me. Stop pushing me away and let me in. Please."

I hate myself for causing the pain and hurt I hear in his voice. My pain is even worse because of it. Closing my eyes, I shake my head and he gently takes my arms in his hands, turning me to face him. Even though rain is dripping from his hair down his face, I can still see the emotional moisture in his eyes–eyes that are saying so much right now.

"Why do you run away from me, darlin'? Why won't you let me love you?"

From deep inside, a sob forces it way to the surface. "Because . . ." I shake my head, unable to say the words, afraid to tell him the secret I've kept from him. Either way, I know I will lose him, but I can't let the words pass through my lips.

"Tell me, Capri. Just tell me, honey." I again close my eyes, shaking my head. "Let it go, baby. Just give it to me and I'll throw it away. I promise." His voice cracks with emotion. "It's okay, darlin. Tell me. Just give it to me and I promise I'll throw it away."

Trembling, I manage to look at him. "I . . . I . . ."

"Let it go, darlin."

Swallowing hard, I keep my eyes on his face. Nausea rises inside me, but I push it back. "I . . ." *I can do this. I have to.* "I am an ovarian cancer survivor." I try to keep my voice from shaking. "Three months ago, I had a hysterectomy. I am twenty years old and I . . . I can never have a baby."

"Oh, honey," he says as a tear trails down his face. "I already knew."

I hiccup, which is something that usually occurs when I

have been crying a lot. "You knew?"

"Capri, Seth told me. I thought you knew he did." When I shake my head, he takes my face in his hands. "All this time, you've been holdin' this all in. You think that matters to me? That it would make me love you less?"

"Doesn't it?"

Instead of answering, he reaches out and slowly removes my wig. My immediate self-consciousness quickly fades as he takes a moment to caress the soft, extremely short waves flattened against my scalp. "You're so beautiful," he says, emotion thick in his throat. "So beautiful." Wrapping me in his muscular arms, he presses my body against his, then touches his lips to mine. My quick gasp turns into a breathy sigh when he whispers, "Open to me, darlin'." I do, and the heat of his mouth makes my whole body come alive. His tongue sweeps across mine, the flavor of him sweet, decadent, and completely addictive. I hunger for more and more.

Wrapping my arms around his neck, I let my fingers get lost in his wet hair and his warm embrace tightens. My body melts against the solid planes of his, every inch of me on fire.

"Marry me, Capri," he whispers against my ear before his lips travel to my neck, his mouth hot against my exposed shoulder. "I love you so much, I can barely breathe. Marry me tomorrow."

"I love you too, and I'll marry you right now," I whisper back, raining kisses on his ear, the burning fire inside me kindling anew as a shudder moves through him followed by a low moan. I long to melt into him. He can't hold me close enough. My hands travel over the muscles of his back, slipping underneath his shirt, the heat of his skin surging up my arms and making me feel even more connected to him, like we are two souls in one body.

After a while, we simply hold one another. A moment later, Jagger's raspy voice fills the silence. "You know, if we were married right now, I'd be doin' a better job of keepin' you warm. Of course then we'd be in danger of settin' this old barn on fire."

My giggle is muffled against his chest. "You don't think the rain would help to put it out?"

"Shoot, no! Woman, the fire would be so hot in here, the wood would dry instantly, not to mention the steam that would fry any birds passing overhead."

I laugh, drawing back a little to look into his eyes. "Tell me again that you love me."

"I love you, darlin'. More than anything in this world."

"And I love you."

As I soak in the warmth of his embrace and the passion

of our kisses is renewed, his declaration of love finds a permanent home in my ever-expanding heart. A home built on the solid and sure foundation of all things unconditional.

Epilogue

*L*ounging on the deck of our honeymoon rental house on the Carolina coast, I read over the last part of my letter to Seth.

You were right, Seth. You were right about everything. At last, I've discovered the real me again. Jagger's love helped me to remember, and I will never forget again. He is the most amazing man I've ever known. He helped me rediscover my worth, unconditionally giving me his love, not knowing if it would ever be returned.

We've decided that we will eventually adopt. We have too much love in our hearts to not share it with children. I long to be a mother, and I know things will work out. Of this, I am certain.

Thank you for introducing me to Jagger. Marrying him was one of the greatest things I have ever, or will ever do in my life. I feel like a complete person now. I will always be grateful you were in tune enough with God to know how much I needed love, how much I needed Jagger.

I look up as Jagger exits the house wearing a pair of faded jeans and nothing else. Just looking at him produces riotous butterflies in my stomach, and I know his effect on me will never fade.

You are really mine, my mind repeats over and over as he takes my hand and pulls me up into his arms. I allow my hands to roam over his chest, then move to his hair, burying my fingers in its softness.

"Do you still wanna go for a walk?" he asks before lightly pressing his mouth to mine, his kiss roaming to my neck, lighting a familiar fire inside me.

"I don't know," I answer in a raspy voice.

"We can always go later."

"Okay."

He smiles against my mouth before deepening the kiss, and suddenly I want nothing more than to travel into the promised sweet oblivion that comes with the touch of his hands and the feel of his body sliding against mine as passion explodes between us. "Much later," he murmurs against my skin. "Because I'm just gettin' started loving on you and this might take all day."

"I'm okay with that," I whisper, my breath catching before he steals it with a hot, completely rapturous kiss, sending heat through my entire body, awing me with its intensity.

As my husband–this man I love more than life–lowers me onto the chaise and we quickly become lost in our love for one another, ecstasy consumes, passion explodes, and we find a now familiar home in each other's arms.

A home of wonder, joy and love.

And in that home, we will forever stay.

About J. Adams

J. (Jewel) Adams stays crazy busy with her family and writing. She has written several books in different genres, mainly romance, and is also a motivational speaker to both youth and adult audiences.

She is on the last leg of home schooling her two youngest, and between that and conjuring up new ideas for her books, her brain is completely fried most of the time. She and her husband Sean are the parents of eight children and grandparents to five, which means they are both losing hair, but hey, that's what Rogaine is for,right?

In her spare time (when she has any) she likes to curl up with a good book and a healthy stash of orange Tic Tacs. She and her family reside in Utah.

Jewel loves hearing from her fans, so if you would like to contact her to tell her how much you love her books or give her sympathy for the fried brain, or suggestions for the hair loss problem (for her husband, of course) contact her at jewela40@gmail.com
To check out Jewel's other books, visit her website at
JewelAdams.com
And stop by her blog: **jewelsbestgems.blogspot.com**

Other books by J. Adams/Jewel Adams
Still His Woman
The Legacy
The Wishing Hour
Tears of Heaven
Place In This World
The Journey
Against the Odds
Mercedes' Mountain
Guardian of My Heart
Sweet 21 Birthday Ball

Ebooks
The Wishing Hour
The Legacy
Tears of Heaven
Place In This World: The Sequel to The Journey
The Journey
Mercedes' Mountain
That Kind of Love
The Shelter of His Arms
What the Heart Sees
The Sound of Love

Stories of the Heart
Against the Odds
Guardian of My Heart
Elise's Heart
For Love of Angel
Sweet 21 Birthday Ball